INTRODUCTION:

In the dark forest, under the moon light and through the rolling clouds, a howling could be heard as werewolf shadow emerges, howling and disturbing the night. Then, the rumbling of thunder and the flashes of lightening, goblins, bats, ghosts, witches and black cats are gathered in the hallow eve. A voice could be heard saying;

"We are the Goblins under your bed, hungry for your children to keep us fed! We are the skeletons creeping underground, rattling skin free bones for a clunkily-clunk sound! We are the Witches swishing through the moonlight, casting magic spells and have yet to get one right! We are the jack-O-Laterns lighting up the scene, some of us are smiling, some are scared and some are just plain mean! We are the children playing make believe, house to house in spooky costumes seeking candy to receive! Come together for just one night and discover what monsters there may be, for this we call that special NIGHT is "ALL HALLOWS EVE!"

CHAPTER ONE: SCHOOLS OUT FOR HALLOWEEN!

Mrs. Sweeney enters the classroom, around her are lot of kids including 8-year-old Mitchell, who is wearing a pirate costume for the Halloween, his friend Sally sitting next to him and Jacob, whose hair is always messy. She gives out instructions to all the kids advising them to stay in groups while going for their "trick or treat" for the night. Suddenly, she stops and asks,

"Where is Beth?"

There is a bit of silence before Mitchell responds,

"Mrs. Sweeney, she didn't come home last night and we think she went looking for her parents. Probably taken by the Rong-a long?"

All the other kids burst in to a loud laughing contest. Mrs. Sweeny, trying to wrap her head around what she just heard, manages to shut them up before asking for more clarification.

"The What?"

This time, Sally decides to help with the explanation, stating that it was true. She further states that the Rong-a long is a boy monster that gets very angry during Halloween and sends out a group of witches to gather people for it to make him happy. He cites examples of people who have been disappearing from the town such as the McPhersons', Joey's Dad, and the Robinsons.

She wondered where the kids got to hear of such myth, but she needed to counter it immediately as she thought it would be the best option.

"I'm not sure that's true kids. I find it ridiculous, but I will call her mom later, she may probably be sick, and I guess that is why she could not make it tonight".

Lewis looks at her in support and says,

"I told you so but ya'll won't listen; tell them Mrs. Sweeny".

In response, Mitchell looks at Lewis with a rather mocking face, calling him names such as *Lousy Lewis, Dummy Lewis* and told him he knew nothing. Immediately he said that he was cautioned by Mrs. Sweeny.

Sally then turns to Lewis and asks,

"If we aren't right, then where is Beth?"

Jacob then cuts in,

"She's our good friend and was supposed to give us word if she found clues to the monster's secret place! We had a plan and she left us this note" he says, showing the others a text from Beth that read:

'I left my glasses at the tree house so I'm
going back there tonight to get them. Also, I may have
found something that'll take us to the Rongalong!

On reading it, Lewis turns to the others and says,

"Beth ran away from home or maybe she is skipping class because Mrs. Sweeny knows the type of group Beth is hanging out with".

This statement gets Mitchell, Jacob and Sally angry as they walk out after class and converge at the tree house later on.

CHAPTER TWO: TREE HOUSE FOR CLUES

Mitchell, Sally, and Jacob climb up a tree using a small ladder and into the tree house. Tonight, the moon is fire bright in the sky. Sally, while climbing up the tree speaks,

"I can't stand Lewis! He's such a teacher's pet!" hissing, and further explaining to the others how lousy Lewis was. The rest of the kids agree to this claim by Sally, but Mitchell tells them they do not have to worry about Lewis rather, their main focus should be on the where about of Beth; their friend, who was at the tree house earlier. He turns to them and says,

"We will have to find out what she learned, and I am sure it would lead us to Rong-a long".

They keep looking around and talking about finding clues, ignorant of the fact that Lewis is climbing up the ladder, eavesdropping on their conversation from outside. A couple of minutes later, Sally looks around and soon sees something shiny on the floor.

"Look guys! Beth's glass!" He exclaims.

"Look!" Jacob also exclaims too.

"What is that?" Mitchell asks.

"It's some kind of Egyptian artifact; It's strange" Jacob replies.

They examine the object; it is a pyramid piece with a cutout design and is about the size of a soft ball.

"Where did she get it from?" Mitchell wonders as Sally quickly breaks his line of thought,

"I think I might know where she got it"

"Where would that be?" Jacob and Mitchell reply.

"It's probably from her dad's museum" Sally says.

"What does an old artifact from a museum have to do with a Rong- a long?" Mitchell asks curiously.

"I had always thought of Rong- a long to be a group of witches or something. I am not sure this is a clue" Jacob objects.

We don't know what the Rong-a long is, Jaky. We need to know more details about it" Mitchell says.

"Details like what?" Sally probed.

"Details like what it is. Where it's from and more." He replies.

"Guess the only way we can find her is to go to the museum" Sally reiterates.

Suddenly, Lewis emerges from his hiding place.

"Ummmmmm…. Not so fast" he says.

As Lewis speaks to the boys, a werewolf slowly creeps down from a branch on the tree. The only thing is something about the werewolf seems different. His fur appears blooming, volumizing and frantically puffy. It looks like a Siberian Husky that has just returned from the salon with a 70s disco style Barbra Streisand or Diana Ross curls, only worse. His oversized tongue flaps out of his mouth and his eyes are not frightening but almost cartoonish. The scary part is the werewolf does have FANGS.

"Lousy Lewis!" Sally calls out, but Lewis is so engrossed in taking the artifact from Sally.

"I will be taking that", he says, as he grabs the artifact from Sally.

"So, your missing friend stole this from the museum huh?" He questions.

"Once I report to the police" …he is about to keep ranting when Jacob cuts him short.

"She didn't steal it, Dingbat. It's from her father's museum".

"So, give it back Lew-ass wipe", says Mitchell.

"Listen to your girlfriend, Mitchell. It's better to keep your mouth shut and appear stupid than to open it and remove all doubt. -that's-Mark Twain, but I bet you didn't know that because you don't pay attention in class and probably can't read at a middle school reading level like myself" Lewis says, as he walks over to the window and faces the others in the tree house.

"Well, it looks like I'll be going now and will be the hero of this case" Lewis says, not noticing the werewolf that has emerged from the open window, snatches him; pulling him out. He immediately drops the artifact and screams in fear.

On seeing this, Mitchell, Jacob and Sally cannot help but scream their head off as they cower in to a safe corner. After a few minutes, Mitchell peeks out the window, trying to see where the werewolf has gone.
"It ran off with him! What was it?" He asks Jacob, who then picks up the artifact.
"It feels like Karma" Jacob says as he tosses the artifact up in the air and catches it.
Jacob then turns to the others and says,
"Ya'll knows what else they say? Never turn your back on an opportunity or an open window".
Sally looks afraid and inquires,
"Do you think he's dead?"
"Maybe, I don't know. Maybe we should tell the police? Mitchell retorts.
"Oh! Sure! Yea, Mr. police officer, a kid in our class was yanked out of our tree house by an angry wolfman. Sounds plausible, right?" Jacob says sarcastically.
"Who would believe us?" he adds.
"Well, regardless, we still need to focus on Beth and finding her. Let's go to her dad's museum and check it out" Mitchell said as they climb down the tree house

CHAPTER THREE: THE MUSEUM

A mummy tomb can be seen as the three friends enter the museum. Significantly, a giant ceiling fan is turning above the mummy tomb. The three friends look around for a while before they eventually see what they are looking for.

"There it is" Jacob says.

Mitchell quickly taps him, as Sally brings out the artifact. She looks at the tomb and notices it has the same shape as the artifact.

"This must be the key to open it" she says as she walks to the tomb

"Wait!" exclaimed Jacob and Mitchell.

"What is it?" She asks in a low tone.

"Dou you think this is a good idea? We don't know what is in there" Mitchell says, looking cautiously.

"What if it is all gruesome, decayed and horrific? You know I would be scarred for life"
Jacob adds, trying not to get near the tomb.

Sally cannot help but laugh sarcastically.

"I'm sure you'll survive. Besides, you guys don't really believe in folklore, ghost stories and monsters coming to life on Halloween" she laughs.

"Well, even if we never did, now we do!" Both Mitchell and Jacob respond.

Sally walks to the tomb to open it, when Lewis rushes in shouting,

"Stoop!!!"

On turning to see who it is, the werewolf and Lewis walks into the museum.

"Lewis! What are you doing here?" Mitchell asks.

"We thought you were dead?" Jacob inquires.

This time, the others take a good look at what the creature is that had snatched Lewis. They notice it looks more like a coyote.

"How are you here with him? We thought you were dead" Sally keeps hammering on that fact.

"It's kind of a long story" Lewis replies.

As he responds, the Werewolf gestures for Lewis to say something.

Lewis then turns to them and says,

"He wants me to tell you something".

And what could that be? Sally fires back.

"Anyway! Anyway! Says Lewis as he heaves a sigh of relief,

"So, ok, um…" He pauses a bit before he narrates his ordeal to them.

"After he violently snatched me from your treehouse, I thought my life was over. Apparently, I assumed he was going to eat me. But he brought me back here and ironically as it somehow turns out, he communicates quite well with charades using different tones. It's easy for me to understand because I was always great at charades during family game night. Anyways, I was able to gather that you cannot let the Mummy out" Lewis concludes.

The Coyote man gestures towards the tomb to correct Lewis. But Lewis is not getting a hang of the message from the coyote man which frustrates it as it becomes more animated trying to correct him.

MMMMMM, HMMMMMMMMMMM, MHMMMMMMMM!!! The Coyote man echoes, still trying to gesture towards what he wants Lewis to say.

"You, said hog!? Not slug? Not hog?" Lewis says, confused and frustrated too.

"Rong-a long!" The others said in unison.

"Yes! That's it! The Rong-a whatever" Lewis says with relief in his eyes. The coyote man gestures and brings his hands to his face in despair.

"Anyways, there's some link between this mummy!" Lewis says, as he walks toward the tomb.
"The Rong-a long, a dracoool-ula and apparently there's some evil witches involved" Lewis continues as he keeps explaining what they are getting themselves involved in.

"You mean Dracula?" Mitchell asks.

"No. no. dra-cooooooool-ula". Lewis repeats.

"Wow. That should be the Halloween classics" Jacob says as everyone in the room pauses. Mitchell gave Jacob a look.

"What? Jacob asks, returning Mitchell's look.

"As I was saying….", Lewis continues as coyote man then gestures at himself, grabbing his poof fur coat as if he wants Lewis to explain more.

"Oh, yes! The fur!" Lewis remembers some details.

"Yo! what's with the coat man?" Jacob asks, as the coyote man growls

"Hey man! No offense." Jacob says, raising his hands up in the air.

"So, the witches made a deal with this coyote man. The deal has something to do with silver bullets and protection if they brought him the crown jewel. Obviously, it, uh, didn't go entirely as they planned to perform, so they double crossed him and turned him into this. That's all I could really get from him so far" Lewis concludes.
"He looks like an overgrown Shrub." Observes Jacob. The beast snarls.

"That's actually pretty good. So, why did 'Shrubs' snatch you from the treehouse?" Sally cuts in almost immediately.
Shrubs covers his face with his hands.
 "Sorry" she continues.

"Because I was the one holding the artifact to free the mummy" Lewis responds.
"Maybe it's the crown jewel? or, I guess he wants to free the mummy to destroy the witches? I'm not sure" Lewis adds.
"So, we can't let this mummy free and come to life otherwise it'll join Dracula and kill the Rong-a long?" Mitchell probes further.
"I got it! The witches plan to send out the Rong-a long tonight to get all the little kids and we can't let a mummy, Dracula or a poufy puff wolf get out there or they'll steal his thunder? And we won't get candy tonight or trick or treating tonight because we can't find Beth and we'll be busy dealing with this soap opera days of our desperate ghouls instead. Pretty good huh" Jacob reiterates sarcastically.
Sally turns to the rest and sits on a chair facing them, while backing the tomb. She is confused.
"I still don't understand what this mummy and those monsters have to do with Beth! "
As soon as she asks the question, there is a screech behind her as the mummy raises its arms as it comes alive. Sally looks back, sees the mummy and screams as the mummy wraps its arms around her.
"Sally!!!" Mitchell and Jacob scream at the same time as they rush off to help her.
They struggle to pull the mummy away from, Sally.

"Get off of her! Coyote, Lewis! Help us!" They both cried while trying to drag the mummy. After a couple of seconds, the mummy shrugs them away and using that opportunity, Sally breaks free. Shrubs then steps in between Sally and the mummy, growling. Both parties burst into a fight, and the mummy manages to throw Shrubs into a pillar holding a giant vase. It crashes onto his head, and he is knocked unconscious. Jacob quickly finds some loose and wraps it behind the mummy.

"Throw it into the ceiling fan!" Mitchell cries out.

Jacob tosses the loose wrap up into the fan, the mummy gets lifted into the air; making a loud bang as it dangles from the fan, wrapped in faded purple bandage.

"Please, no! Don't suck me up into the blades" A voice says. They all stop and are surprised. Sally is the first to speak up.

"You're a ...you're a woman?" She asks.

"Were you expecting king tut?" The mummy replies.

"Sort of., so who are you?" Sally asks.

"I'm his mum" the mummy replies.

"His mum!" They all exclaim.

"You're British?" Jacob asks.

"That is very observant of you dear". The mummy replies.

"Whose mom, are you?" Sally probes.

"Ronnie's." The mummy replies.

"Whos-ohhhhhhhh. Rong-a long has a mum. I got it now!" Jacob exclaims.

"Wait. What's a female British mummy doing in an Egyptian pharaoh's tomb? That's a mother to an estranged Rong-a long creature?" Mitchell asks as Lewis still stands in shock.

"My name is Ava Smith. I was an archeologist from the 1900s and in 1903. I was carrying out research when I discovered the tomb. I found a spell and said it out loud. Then, somehow, I switched places with the pharaoh" The Mummy narrates how it came to be.

"Bad move" Jacob cuts in.

"Yes. Anyway, as I was saying, Ronnie is my son and you must help me to find him," the mummy continues.

If you're the Rong-a long's mom, then who's his dad?" Mitchell inquires.

"You, beast" said Jacob, as he turns around and looks at unconscious Shrubs.

"I'm afraid not. I'll tell you more if you help me down and we really should leave before he wakes up" the mummy cuts in.

"How do we know you are his mom and that is your real reason for wanting to find him? This beast claims you would come alive and destroy it?" Sally queries.

Meanwhile, Lewis has come out of his shock and finally speaks.

"Correct. The fur ball told us your intentions are to hurt the Rong a-long and his witches. It would be bad if you got out".

"What do you think you guys? Should we cut her down?" Sally asks.

They quickly huddle up. Then, Sally comes out of the huddle and says,

"We need a reason; a really good reason".

"How 'bout, a mummy's love?" The mummy replies.

"A mummy's love!? Nope!!! Sorry! I was looking for something more like

"I promise not to kill you and your friends when I'm down... that sort of thing you know. In fact, I say we fan her!" Jacob exclaims as he gets ready to flip the switch.

"Quiet Jacob! So, tell us about a mummy's love" Sally asks.

The mummy pauses for a bit before saying,

"A MUMMY'S LOVE. It is the greatest love that can never be broken. Forever real with such great appeal, and it exists even if unspoken. I wanted that feeling before my curse of falling to pharaoh's tomb. But when I found myself in a full wrap, I felt almost certainly doomed. I'd never be able give that Mummy's love to my child's gentle soul in need, instead, I'd rot in a cold dark tomb, under the horses feed. But then one day, we found a way as I met an unconventional man".

As the mummy was talking, her bones cackle.

"A charming soul that wanted the same and together we had a plan. There was a mad scientist to most people, but to me, he was a doctor of good will; a miracle worker of absolute genius and of the greatest skill" she continues.

"A year later, RONG A LONG was taken to the witches because his baritone singing voice makes the witches young and beautiful" she says, heaving a sigh.

"Wait. How does this wolfman come into play?" Sally cuts in.

"I don't understand. What did it tell you?" The mummy asks.

"He said that it has something to do with a Dracoolula and a bunch of witches?" Sally replies.

"Witches? Could it be?....... We must go see the doctor. If we're to have any chance at finding the count, he'll know where he is" the mummy responded.

"What do we do about the wolfman?" Mitchell asks.

"Shrubs, you mean?" Lewis clarifies.

"And what do we do about him?" Jacob asks as he gestures towards Lewis.

"He's coming with us. You say he knows how to communicate with the wolf? Well, after we find the count, we'll come back and talk with the wolf if he is awake and see if he might know where these witches live" The mummy replies.

"Good idea. Let's at least detain him so when he awakes, he's not going anywhere" Mitchell affirms.

"Any idea on where to detain him?" Sally asks.

Mitchell and Jacob eye the Tomb, before Mitchell speaks up

"We can put him in there! We have the key" he said.

"Sure, but I don't know about that" Lewis says.

Jacob turns to Lewis and asks for him to hold up Shrubs.

They drag Shrub's giant limp body and place it upright in the tomb. As they turn for a brief moment to get the door, Shrub's face plants out onto the ground on top of Lewis.

"Get him off!" Lewis shouts.

"I said hold him!" Jacob argues as they lift him back up, place him in the tomb and lock him up.

"Perfect. Let's get going. We should be back hopefully before he wakes and starts howling drawing attention to himself" the mummy says and walks towards the door of the museum.

Boo

CHAPTER FOUR: THE MOUTACHE'S LAB

Sally, Jacob, Mitchell, Lewis, and the Mummy all sit in an office awaiting the good doctor's arrival. The Doctor's office is a blend between the old classic Frankenstein's lab and an OB-GYNs office. There are giant pictures on the walls of ugly beastly babies, monster looking children, and a line of oversized medical tools, comical to say the least. The Mummy is trying as much as she can to stay awake. They soon break into a conversation to keep the mummy awake.

"Explain it to me again? We're in this um, office, to see a doctor that was responsible for making the Rong-a long through an experiment between you and Dracula?" Sally probes.

"Dra-coooool-ula. Sally. Not Dracula" Jacob corrects.

"Yes. He and I wanted to have a baby, but the Drac could not, ya know" The mummy says.

"Anyway, Dr. Moustache, was well known in OB-GYNSS" She continues.

"OBGYNSS?" Mitchell cuts in.

"ODD BABIES AND GHOULS YOU NEVER SHOULD SEE" says the Mummy

"I see. Well, whatever you do, don't fall asleep" Sally warns.

"I'll try my dear but I'm so very tired. An odd ball nurse enters the room!" The mummy replies.

Soon, a nurse walks, stands by the door and says,

"Hallo! May I present..... DOC-TORRRRRRRR MOUSSS TASHHHHHH!" She elongates the name for emphasis.

Dr, Mustache walks into the office. A goofy presence. He is a very old senile goof with wild hair and an oversized mustache. He has thick medical glasses that bulges his eyes. His lab coat is worn, oversized and he is about five feet tall. His assistant nurse is large.

"HALLO!" The Doctor says as he walks in and takes his seat.

"I am Doctor Moussssstache!" He says, just before the Mummy collapses over on the patient's table.

"What in God's name have we here!? The doctor exclaims.

Sally at first assumes the Doctor is referring to Mummy sitting on the patient table, but he passes the mummy by and heads straight for Lewis. Even when Sally tries explaining to him the reason for bringing the mummy along, the doctor ignores.

He looked at Lewis and says,
"Ahhhhhh my dear boy! Ze Wrong a longgg has grown up and becomes a sure magnificent creature! So horrendous!" He exclaims, takes a pause and continues.

"I am brilliant! I've done it again, another creation of sheer abomination!"

"What!? I'm not!" Lewis protests.

"Shhh shhh shh, my dear boy! It must've been very hard for you to adapt to ze normal children of the world. Your head so misshaped, your voice so evil and wretched. I can only promise you; it does not get any better" the doctor says as he advances near Lewis.

"I'm not the Rong-a long! I'm Lewis" he says as he pushes the doctor back.

"Oh! Of course. I knew that" the doctor replies.

He walks over to Jacob and whispers,

'Those poor parents".

"Tell me about it" Jacob says.

"Hey, what's this?" Jacob inquired as he finds a strange looking leather belt about 8 ft long that has some mechanics built into it. Sort of like a giant dog collar.

"Don't touch that!" the doctor says.

"It's a voice translator, very useful for many monster creatures that cannot speak. It translates their monstrous groans to English or Spanish" he adds.

"Cool!" Jacob replies to him as he turns it on and places it to his throat.

"Hola, Donde esta caramelo?" Jacob says.

"Put that down!" The doctor exclaims this time. Jacob then places it on the patient's table.

"Dr! Please!" Sally begins.

"Of course! Of course! Let me refocus. Yes! So, you are here, why?" He asked

"We found this mummy, who happens to be the "Mommy" of a very important creature named a Rong-a long that we think has our friend, that you apparently created many years ago for a desperate Mummy and sterile ice-cold count. The baby then vanished and was probably taken by the count! So, we need to find this count so we can find this monster and get our friend and her parents back! We need to find the Count" Mitchell says.

"This ice-cold count? He had a low count?" The doctor inquires.

"What did you say?" Sally, asks, trying to get what the doctor said.

"Only ones with low count, right here" Jacob says, pointing to his candy bag as he empties the bag, but no candy falls out.

"It is of no consequence. Anyway, I cannot give out such information. Only to a direct family member with consent who was there for the experiment can I give such info" the doctor replies.

"Look Doc. we need you to revive this Mummy" Sally says, pointing to the mummy.

"She was there! If you wake her up, then we can find Dracoooula and learn what happened to their boy" she concludes.

"I'm sorry, but I do not do charity work. I will need some form of payment. Do you have insurance?" The doctor says, putting his hands forward.

"What? no? There should be no form of payment" Sally says.

"Well," the doctor replies,

"Perhaps we can come to sort of deal. If you would be willing to listen to my song about ze hardships of this medical life, this ambassador of science and creation! I will then perform the procedure" he adds.

Despite it, the children agreed with disdain.

"Wonderful!" The doctor said with excitement as he began to sing.

As the doctor sings, Jacob and Mitchell notices a machine nearby the Mummy showing energy. They are messing around with it playfully as kids would and are playing catch with an electric wand attached to a cord. Jacob misses a catch and the wand lands on the Mummy. The Mummy feels it and gets up. There is a big zap! Something ZAPPED, a loud flash and bang! The mummy is revived. As the Mummy is revived, she kicks The DOG COLLAR VOICE TRANSLATOR into JACOB'S HALLOWEEN TRICK OR TREAT BAG.

"Whoa whoa, thanks Doc., but we got her. No need for the song" Jacob says.

"Excellent! Now. Remind me of the time?" The doctor asks.

"Dr. Don't you remember when Dracool-ula and I came to see you about a century ago and you made for us the Rong-along?" The mummy asks.

"Indeed. What an experiment! Combine a mummy with a Dracula! How grotesque!" The doctor says.

"How is the creature?" He asks.

"He vanished". The mummy replies.

"Gasp! As I figured, he would" The doctor says.

"With the Count!" The mummy reiterates.

"Ah. I see. I never saw that coming. Men of utter darkness, you can never count of them. Be careful because whomever lives near this Rong-a long will have absolute power" The doctor responds.

"Absolute power?" Jacob asks.

"Well, almost absolute. His gift amplifies energy and whomever is near engulfs it, grows powerful themselves from it. So, Dracula's powers could be unheard of now" The doctor answers, laying emphasis on the power of Dracula.

"I need to find them. Can you give me an updated address where the Count might be living today?" The mummy asks eagerly.

"We might" the doctor says and calls out to the nurse.

"Nurse!".

"Yes! Doctor!" the nurse answers from the doorway.

"Do you remember the case.... of... hmmmm... the mummy and dracoolula and their..... Rong-along!??" the doctor asks, trying to allow the nurse figure it out; as both doctor banter back and forth playfully.

"Of course, doctor!" The nurse replies.

"Why are they yelling?" Jacob inquires.

"And do you have in ze file where the count's current address is!?" The doctor asks.

"Absolutely doctor!" She says, yelling back her answers to the doctor.

"Give us ze address please!" The doctor asks in his German like tongue.

"No!" the nurse replies.

"No!? Why, no?" All three of the kids ask at the same time.

"You don't know!?" The doctor asks.

No, no. the address is "know" I don't know it" the nurse says.

"Nurrrrrse! The doctor yells.

"You give ussssss that address now!" He says in an extremely loud voice.

I don know!! she yelled back

"Let me see that" Jacob says,

"It says "five down grove".

"Well, that was unnecessary" Sally said sarcastically.

"Let's go you guys" she said.

"zanks for coming by!" The doctor says as the rest walk out of the lab.

CHAPTER FIVE: THE STREETS OF TRICK OR TREAT

The children walk down a street to the entrance of a cul de sac, with the Mummy. They are looking for the Count's address. Many other kids in costumes pass them by and are out tricking or treating back and forth door to door. Every house is well decorated and lit.

"Ah man! This is what we should be doing. Trick or Treating" Jacob says, looking at the other kids walk by.

"Look at all the fun they're having!" He speaks.

"Look at this way, you've seen more real monsters and ghouls tonight than any of these kids have" Sally reminds him.

"Yea, but with real fears and no candy". Jacob answers her.

"You're going to become borderline diabetic man." Mitchell comments.

"Personally, I never understood this concept of Trick or Treating? Kids go to strangers' doors and just ask for Candy?" She asks Jacob.

"You're over thinking it. What's to understand?" Jacob replies to her.

"Yea, but where did it come from?" Mitchell inquires, wanting to know the origin of the celebration.

"It's based on old Celtic traditions from about 2,000 years ago. They lived in the old countries of what is today Ireland, UK and France. They would leave food out and dress is costume to scare away evil spirits. Then later on, it turned into 'MUMMING'" The mummy tutors her.

"Mumming? Is that how you came to be popular in it?" Jacob inquisitive nature kicks in.

No. Mumming was in the culture where people dressed as ghosts, other creatures and performed antics then in exchange for food or drink. Later became known as "ALL HALLOWS EVE" a religious context the day before all saint's day that has probably now become your modern day "Trick or Treating" The mummy explains further.

"Oh, I always just thought Charlie Brown started it with their Halloween episode. Which is a really good one by the way?" Jacob says in a happy tone.

"Who?" The mummy asks, wanting to know more about the subject Jacob just talked about.

"Never mind him. So, you really think this Count is the same one from a century ago? Didn't you say he ran off and left you?" Sally asks, wanting to know the fact.

"Are there other Counts?" Jacob interrupts.

"I'd hate to believe it's true, but yes" the mummy replies to them.

As they are speaking, a strange kind of storm emerges, accompanied by FLASHES OF LIGHTNING, SOUND OF THUNDER and WIND. They can hear the laughter of witches as they approached from the sky.

"This is not good!" Mitchell says as she looks around her

Finally, the witches land in the background behind a house.

"HAHA ITS ABOUT TO GET WORSE!" One of the witches said.

Jacob turns to the rest and says,
"Quick, run into that house!"

All of them make a run for the nearest door, but as they almost get the door, the WITCHES POP OUT FROM INSIDE!

"Not so fast!" Says one of the witches named Murina, that seems to be the leader of the coven.

The kids jumped back toward the street.

"What have we here!?" says Murina.

"Looks like an old bag of bones free from a tomb" replies one of the witches making emphasis of the mummy.

"Oh my, and she's made some new friends. Good for a stew perhaps" another one of the witches says.

"What do you want?" Mitchell fires at them with sparkle of fire in her eyes.

"We're looking for a pet of ours, harry little beast. Lost his way. About yay high, fangs, kind of harebrained! We heard was last seen with some sneaky children and a Mummy? Why are you here old miss Mum? Curious. You should not have any reasons" says the leader of the coven.

"She's looking for her son! Ronnie" Sally jumps to the defense of the mummy.

"Quiet young blood, the dead speaks with the dead. Speak again and I'll remove your tongue!" Murina says in a wicked tone.

"But!" Sally tries to cut in, but the Murina turns around and casts a spell on her; Sally could no longer speak. The more she tries to speak, the more she murmured.

"Sally! Oh my God! You took her voice!" Jacob and Mitchell say at the same time.

"I ask you again MUM, what purpose do you have here from the tomb?" Murina asks as she once again turns towards the mummy.

"These children woke me from my sleeping place and now, I seek to find my boy. He's been missing for some time" the mummy replies.

As she is replying, the other two witches circle around the children as both the mummy and leader of the coven speak.

"Maybe we can help? What does this creature look like?" Murina asks, trying to get more information.

"Like, a Rong a long" The mummy replies.

Some of the witches gasp!

"Hmmmm, we have not seen such creature in this town. Have we girls?" The leader of the witches says and turns around to ask the rest.

"Noooo. Noooo. None around here" the other witches reply.

"You lie!" Mitchell says abruptly.

FROG- OATEM- CROAKS- IT! Says the leader of the coven of witches and instantly, Mitchell becomes a giant frog monster with same pants and little vest. He is ribbiting as Jacob calls out his name 'Mitchell in horror.

"Anything to add young man?" The leader of the witches turns to Jacob and asks, but Jacob stays silent and looks away.

"Didn't think so" says the leader before he turns to the mummy and speaks.
"Again, I'm sorry my mal nourished bag of dust. We haven't seen such a creature but we will keep an eye out. Now on your way, poor Mum lost in the modern world. For you will not find anything else of value here. Be on your way, do it not and that tells me you want trouble from us and YOU don't want trouble from us. Understood miss mug-a-bones?""

"That's a tempting offer, but I must decline" says the mummy.

"So be it" the leader of the coven says, turns to the rest of the witches and speaks.

"Ladies, the skinny wrap wants to see what happens when you cross a witch's power. Let's show them!"

The witches all laugh and begin their exercise in power. They surround the kids and mummy. Plumes of smoke begin to rise. As lightning and thunder roar and lit up in the sky, the Leader of the witches zaps the Mummy with some purple light from her hand. The Mummy as a result falls to her knees. The witches swoop in for their attack, but are stopped by an approaching figure that emerges from the house next door.

"Witches Stop!" Says the approaching figure which came in to the light of the night and it was Dracula, as the figure walked a blast of cold snow filled the area and the witches retreated in fear.

"Ah, The Count, has arrived" says the leader of the witches as she turns around to see who the figure is.

"Your powers do not supersede our Count! Mind your affairs!"

"Would you like to find out Witch!?" The Count asks.

"I could turn you all to ice and cast you to the tundra of the North, buried under a mountain of snow never to be thawed or found" he says with a nit of frankness in his tone.

After a few minutes of pondering, the leader of the witches, turns to the rest of the coven and says,

"Come ladies! We have business elsewhere. This isn't over MUM"

 Then she turns to the mummy and says,

"I don't want to see you here again".

"Before we go, you said I could get one child for a stew tonight" one of the witches says, suddenly grabs Lewis and then flies off.

"Help! Why does this keep happening to me!" Lewis shouts to the rumbling of thunder and lighting.

"Wow, that was close. Thanks so much sir" Jacob says.

Dracula turns to Jacob and asks

"I'm sorry but what about your friend that was taken?"

"Oh, that's just Lewis. He'll be fine". Jacob replies.

"They just said they plan to make a stew out of him? Are you sure? Should we go and save him?" Dracula inquires.

"mmmmm, nope. He's ok" Jacob replies.

"Ok then. And, what's with the toad?" Dracula asks as the Monster toad waves towards Jacob.

"Oh that's my buddy Mitchell. Witches turned him into that because he was mouthing off to them and took Sally's voice for the same reason. We'll probably have to go to their place at some point to get that stuff fixed. But I kind of like his new look though; wonder what kind of vertical he could get for basketball? Anyway, reason we're here" Jacob says.

Dracool-ula notices Mummy on her knees struggling to get up.

"Mum!?" Dracula says in astonishment.

"Hello Count" the mummy says weakly.

CHAPTER SIX: DRACOOLULA'S QUARTERS

"My goodness, what happened! Come, let's get you into my house" Dracula say as he leads the way to his house. He leads the way to the entrance of his house, as they follow the count into the main hall.

The place is cold and frigid, like an ice cube with many icicles. Dracula is cold blue and wears sunglasses. He is blue with snow frozen on him and his furniture is made of ice blocks. There is a type writer, papers everywhere and many books.

"I'm thirsty, I need a Drink" Dracula says.

Jacob places both hands over his neck and speaks

"It's bad blood trust me! I'm O negative.

Dracula gives a little laugh and says,

"I don't drink human blood boy. I'm an artic count. You're thinking of my cousin from the north. Draculas drink blood, I drink hmmm.. He says, thinking of what the substance is called. Suddenly, his eyes pop up.

"Ice Tea! He finally says.

Jacob takes a deep sigh of relief. The count is about is business but soon turns to Jacob and asks.

"Does your toad need flies or water or anything?"

"Flies might be good. Mitch, you want dinner buddy?" Jacob asks as the count releases some flies into the room. The toad monster does its best to slap them with its giant tongue but misses a lot.

"Anyway. You are here? How did you get here?" The Count asks.

Sally tries to explain but cannot say nothing as the only thing that can escape from her mouth is hmmming. The count then gives her a cold drink moments later.

"Here, drink this. It'll reverse the voice spell and your voice will come back. You might groggy a little bit" he says.

Sally clears her throat and speaks

"Tell him, Mummy".

"Is Ronnie here?" The mummy asks.

"Why would he be here?" Dracula replies.

"Well, let me see. You took him you frosty Bas-" the mummy tries to talk but is soon cut off by Sally who decides to put it straight to the count.

"She means! She means she thinks, she has reason to believe those many years ago you up, left and took your son with you" Sally says.

"And put her back in the tomb" Mitchell adds.

"What's a frosty Bas...?" Jacob asks.

"Dude, stay focused" Sally replies him.

"That's what you think? I ran off with our son and put you into a tomb?" Dracula replies.

"You guys it doesn't help fighting". Sally says.

"I came home that day from ice fishing and everyone was gone" Dracula says with a bit of choke in his voice as if he wants to cry.

"Catch anything good?" Jacob asks.

"Few trout and some bass" Dracula replies.

"Anyway" the mummy replies.

"Anyway. As I was saying. I came home, you were gone, Rong-a long was gone and there was a note that said,

"I'm leaving you Drac, you're just too cold and boring and I'm taking Ronnie too" I was heartbroken and confused!

"I was in the tomb! You didn't bother to check the tomb!?" The mummy fired back.

"Why would you be in the tomb? Why are you back in there? How on earth did you end up in the tomb and not realize it?" Dracula asks with a bit of anger in his voice.

"So, you didn't take him?" The mummy asks, trying to clarify.

"No. I have no clue where he is. I fell into a big depression, sold the castle and moved here to work on my novel" Dracula says with sadness in his eyes and tone.

"Oh cool, you're writing a novel? What's it about?" Jacob asks inquisitively.

"Jakky!" Sally says, trying to call Jacob to order.

"What.?" He replies her

Sally grabs the unpublished manuscript. She reads the title out loud "COUNT DOWN TO ZERO HOUR: a Vampire's loss"

"That sounds uplifting" Jacob says.

"You've been working on this for almost a hundred years and still aren't done?" Sally asks, sarcastically.

"I get easily distracted and have moments of writers block" Dracula replies her while the Toad monster Mitchell continues to catch flies.

"Look, that's beside the point, okay? So you just went to writing? Not even a moment to look for us?" Mummy questions the Count.

"I spent decades looking around the world for the two of you. It's actually how I came to be here in this town because I heard tales of a Rong-a long creature" The Count replies her.

"So you didn't leave us" The mummy says as she hugs the Count.

"So, if it wasn't you who took Ronnie, and you don't know where he is, this puts us back at square one in our search to find Beth" Sally says, distorted and disgruntled.

"And possibly Lewis. Wait! Lewis and the werewolf! If we go back to the museum maybe we could get more info out of the wolf- "says Jacob but is cut off from finishing what he had to say by Sally who had a point to make.

"Only Lewis knew how to communicate with it, Jacob and he's gone" Sally says.

"What did this wolf tell you?" Dracula inquires.

"He said that he brought Lewis to the museum to free the mummy to get revenge against the witches for something a bad spell" Sally replies.

"Yea. A deal gone wrong" Jacob adds.

"A deal?" Dracula asks.

"Yea, I don't know all the details. If the wolf were here, he could better explain it" Jacob says.

Suddenly there is a howling in a distance and soon Shrubs pops up out of a cave like looking window above from on top the house.

"He escaped! And somehow, he's found us here?" Jacob says, afraid as the fear could be heard in his voice.

"Stand back everyone!" Dracula says as shrubs makes his way down to them. He gestures to them he's not there to hurt them, but to help.

"No, we will not give you Mitchell as a treat" Jacob tells him.

"Something about the witches?" The mummy asks shrubs.

"This is going to take forever". Sally says as shrub is frustrated. Sally sits down on the chair where Jacob had placed his bag earlier.

"What the..." she exclaims.

"What is it? Oh, my bag" Jacob asks.

"It's obviously nothing" Jacob replies her.

"No. There's" Sally counters.

She opens the bag and speaks

"What's this!?"

"Oh no way! That's the voice translator from Dr Moustache's office! It must've fallen in there when we were dealing with Mummy!" Jacob replies.

"Hm. Does it work? Sally asks.

"I don't know. The doc told me that's what it's used for" Jacob answers.

"Let's give it a shot" the mummy says as she walked towards Shrubs.

"Ok, we put this on" she says, as Shrubs nods in agreement as they put the device on him.

"Hello? Hello? It works" Shrubs says.

"That's great!" Jacob comments.

"Can you tell us where our boy is? Where is the Rong-along?" Mummy asks Shrubs

"Well. Where do I begin" Shrubs says.

He tells the party that his name was Roy and he has been a werewolf for 200 years. He also tells them how he was approached by the witches in the 1930s to a deal. He then explains ro them how the witches had informed him to snatch a newborn baby from a couple of monsters in Europe and bring the child here and they would in turn give him a spell of protection and a silver bullet proof fur coat, which would make him invincible.

"Yes, it was I who took your Rong-along. I am sorry" Shrubs says with regret in his eyes.

"Busted!" Jacob shouts.

"When I returned to the witches' cottage, they had deceived me and instead of getting my fur of protection, they gave this" Shrubs says as he points to his fur coat.

"Why would they want Ronnie?" The mummy asks.

"Something he has, gives them power and youth. I don't know what it is. but he's been with them ever since" Shrubs explains.

"Why didn't you get the baby back after the spell? Dracula asks.

"The spell took away my hunt instincts and made into this ridiculous floof. I was shamed by my community of wolves and went into hiding. I spent most of my time grooming. It wasn't until recently I heard someone was looking for the Mummy that I decided to come out" Shrub says with a bit of resentment in his voice.

"So then, you know where the witches live!?" Sally queries.

"I do and I know of an entrance on the roof where we can sneak in, but to get past the pumpkin guard, you need to know the answer to the riddle" Shrubs answers her.

"What's the answer? Dracula asks.

"It's...." Shrubs says and all they could hear was BZZZT BZZZZT BZZZZT. The voice box shorts out and Shrubs just howls.

"Perfect. Hope someone here is good at riddles" Jacob cuts in.

"Let's go you guys! We're wasting time! Wolfman, show us how to get to the witches' cottage!" Sally says as they step out of the house in to the dark.

SUB ZERO
BOO

CHAPTER SEVEN: THE GATE OUTSIDE THE COTTAGE:

The witches' coven is located up on the hillside with the road leading up to it. As the party walks uphill to the location, they discover it is an old forest with pumpkin patches, a giant IRON GATE keeping out residents. With TWO MASSIVE PUMPKINS "GUARD" at the gate. The group approaches the gate, and PUMPKIN GUARD ONE immediately comes to life, walks to the group and speaks.

"Stop! No one dare enters!"

"Only those who can answer the 3 riddles may enter through the gate". The second Pumpkin guard adds.

"What are they?" Sally inquires.

"All others must turn back!" Says one of the guards.

"We got it. What's the riddle" Jacob asks.

"You get three tries per riddle! Answer right and enter away, answer wrong and someone dies" says one of the pumpkin guards.

"Wait you just said others turn back?" Jacob asks again.

"I think they mean if we accept the challenge" The mummy replies.

"Are you ready to proceed?" One of the guard asks.

"We accept. We're ready" Sally says.

"She's speaking for herself. It's a one by one situation right? Not a group thing?" Jacob inquires.

"Hush" The mummy says, trying to *shhhh* Jacob

The Pumpkin guard starts to move, float in rhythm, then turns to the group and says,

"I have no feet to dance, I have no eyes to see I have no life to live or die, but yet I do all three. What am I?

"Anyone?" Sally asks.

"You're fire!" Dracula echoes.

"Wow, great job!" The others say.

"Riddle 2," said the pumpkin guard.

"The person who built it, sold it. The person that bought it never used it and the person who used it, never saw it. What is it?" He asked.

"A blind man's cane?" Sally asks.

"Incorrect. Two more tries" says the pumpkin guard.

"You're a pair of concert tickets?" Says Jacob.

"What!?" Sally inquires.

"Incorrect. Last try or you die" says the pumpkin guard.

"I got it! You're a coffin!" Mummy says.

"Correct" says the pumpkin guard.

"Great job!" Dracula comments.

"Last one" says the pumpkin guard.

"How do you spell Candy in two Letters?"

"Oh man! This is right up my alley! I got this!" Jacob says.

"What's a candy that's too letters?" Sally asks.

"That's impossible" Dracula utters.

"Wait...wait. I think he's got it" The Mummy says.

"C AND Y" says Jacob.

"Correct. You all may enter" says the pumpkin guard.

Everyone cheers Jacob as they enter through the gate.

"As if that wasn't hard enough, now we have angry witches to deal with next" Jacob commented on their way in.

The cottage is an old and run down, with dark wood walls, flooring and tree branches used as joists for the roof. The place is filled with all typical witches' accessories, furniture, brooms, potions, cauldrons, etc. Stairs go up on one side of the backwall, to an open balcony space that ran the length of the house left to right. The group enters quietly through the left side and gets into the main living room.

There is a divider wall in the middle of the living room and on the left side the parents are in a large jail cell. A giant black bag hangs near a fireplace and strangely, it is moving.

"I think there's something in there" Dracula says, as whatever was in the bag mumbled. Sally and Jacob rushes to open the bag and Lewis falls out. Dracoolula puts out the fire with his ice spells, while the Wolf and Mitchell looks around the room. The Mummy on the other hand, hangs tight on the rooftop.

"It's Lewis!" Jacob exclaims.

"Lousy Lewis. We thought you were dead" Sally whispers to him.

"They were about to make me for beef stew" Lewis responds.

"A moment later and you would've been" Jacob jokes about it.

"Come on. Where are the witches?" Have you seen Beth or anyone else?" Sally asks.

"I don't know. I heard voices earlier from that hall?" Lewis says as Jacob takes a look.

"These stairs go down! Shrubs, lead the way". Jacob says.

"Why don't you go? I've seen what these witches can do. I'm in no hurry to lose something else too" Shrubs says suddenly as the voice translator comes up again.

"I'll go first. I can match their spells with my own. You two help her down first. Stand back" Dracula says.

He makes a glowing blue light and walks down the stairs. Jacob is wowed by the glowing blue light.

"Follow me" Dracula said.

The group follows Dracula down the steps to the basement. They enter a vast crypt and the crypt is grand in scale filled with concrete pillars that supports the vaulted ceilings and the room seems to go on forever. It is lit up by many cauldron fires hanging from the pillars, close by a giant iron jail cell filled with many of the lost parents, and Beth!

"It's Beth!" Sally cries.

They rush over the cell door.

Sally, Jacob and Mitchell cannot hold back their joy as they whisper her name.
"Beth!"

Beth looked up, she was obviously very weak and tired. Beth replied huh?

"Beth! it's us! it's Sally! And Jake and Mitch! Wake up!" Sally shouts.

"Sally? Sally! Oh my god! How did you get here? Oh thank God! Please get us out of here! The witches will be back soon, probably with another group of parents". Beth laments.

"Why did the witches bring you all in here?" Jacob inquires.

"They said it was for the creature boy. The wrong a thing" Beth replies.

"Rong-a long" Jacob and Sally say.

"Where is he? Where is Ronnie?" The mummy asks.

"Why is there a pink mummy?... Beth asks.

"I don't know. They keep him somewhere else in the crypt. They said they need to keep bringing in new groups of parents, because he gets happy for a moment and sings for them, but then realizes it's not the right group of parents. So, he sings somberly and they get angry" she explains.

"Why does he need to sing for them? that's odd" Jacob comments.

"For their powers. His singing re-energizes their powers" Dracula answers.

"But his somber tune weakens them. He knows. He needs his true mum and..." the mummy said but Dracula cuts in.

"dad" Dracula says.

"What!? Get me the heck outta here!" Beth says.

"I don't care how you do it. Just get me and my dad out of here" She begs.

"Wait, why did they take Beth? She's not a parent?" Jacob asks curiously.

"Are you serious right now!? I don't know. Can we solve the mystery later!? Before they get back. I was with my dad. I have no clue?" Beth responds.

"They probably thought when she was with her dad that it was another mom and dad and just grabbed them both" Sally answers.

"Don't worry Beth. We'll get ya out. We got this dude" Jacob says as he points to Dracula.

"Can you freeze this lock? Jacob asks.

"I'll try" Dracula says.

"Stand back everyone!" Sally says as Dracula casts a spell and sends ice to the jail cell door. It shatters the hinges and the door opens up. There is a loud monstrous roar and Warf bells ringing.

"Oh no! it's the monster boy! the Rong-a long! He's calling on them! They'll be here soon! We must go!" Beth says in a worried voice.

The Rong-a long comes out of the shadows carrying a weapon of some kind. He's a disfigured creature sharing traits of both Dracula and the mummy. He's half bandaged and half blue, partly skeletal and partly obese, grotesque, and yet somewhat innocent and pathetic.

"Shrubs! kill him!" Jacob says.

"No! Wait! The mummy says, and everyone stands still where they are.

"Ronnie!" The mummy says in a low and lovely tone filled with care and love.

The Rong-a long recognizes the voice, and he lowers his weapon.

"He knows it's her" Dracula says.

"He knows it's both of you. Go see him" Sally urges Dracula. Both Dracula and the mummy approach Ronnie and they all embrace.

"My son" The mummy says in elation.

"Aw. I'm posting this to my Instagram" Jacob says.

"It's finished. We can all go home now" Sally says but is suddenly interrupted by the Leader of the witches.

"Not just yet little miss!" She says as the other witches arrive.

As they come in, one of the witches lands a blow to the back of Dracula's head knocking him down and unconscious.

"Look who it is. Coming to take our property away miss Mugabones. I told you what would happen if you came around again" the leader speaks.

"Rong-a long is not yours! The wolf gave us all the details! You made a deal with him that if he stole the baby of the Drac and mummy he would get full protection against silver bullets in his fur" Jacob counters.

"Which was a lie. I want what was promised me!" Said Shrubs.

"Lies! Why would we need a Rong-a long baby!" The leader of the witches asks.

"Because you heard it would give you infinite powers!" Sally counters.

"I told you we should've killed the wolf" one of the witches murmurs.

"Agreed, but it was so much more fun to turn him into a giant cotton ball at the time" the leader said and sighed.

"My mistake. Ok? We took your son, and now he is ours and here he'll stay and now we have you and the Drac to keep him happy" the leader said with much gusto.

"So now no one is leaving" said another of the witches.

"Yes, no one" added the other.

"First, I will deal with the hair brained mutt! For causing all these troubles. Pup-to-it!" the order came as she made a plume of smoke and Shrubs becomes a small k9 puppy. Jacob picks him up and turns to Sally and speaks.

"What do we do? We need Dracula".

"Run?" Sally asks.

"Everybody, run!" Jacob shouts.

Immediately, everyone outside the jail cell makes a run for it behind pillars and for the shadows. The witches laugh hysterically.

"Silly children. Nowhere to run! ex stillem a momentum anthropos!" The leader of the witches says and everyone freezes in place where they are.

"Gather them up girls" She instructs the others as one by one, the other witches put the people back into the jail cell. First the mummy, then Jacob. As the third witch starts to bring Sally in, she turns to Dracula and screams,

"No!" Drac wake up!".

The leader of the witches laughs and says,

"Oh yea, count snow cone" He's had his last cold bite.

She turned to Drac and speaks.

"Grand ohferum a- " But she is cut short by Mitchell who swings in by his tongue and crashes into the leader of the witches knocking her off her broom and into Dracula, who gets woken up by the crash.

"Mitchell! He's not human so the frozen spell must've not worked on him! Get them dude! yea!" Jacob cheers him on as he continues to cause havoc amongst the witches. Soon, the group cheered from inside the cell.

"Get that toad! Get him!" The leader of the witches says angrily. The other witches charge at him but he leaps away from them.

"Yea! Look at that vertical! Jacob says as Dracula gets to his feet.

"To tundra!" Dracula yells. A loud bang alongside winds, and soon the witches are gone. Mitchell turns human again and Shrubs becomes himself again.

"Where are they?" Beth inquires.

"I sent them to the tundra of the north. Frozen in about a mile deep of ice" Dracula replies her.

"It's all over and we have our boy back! Our Rong-a long" The mummy says.

They all make it out of the witches' coven and back in time to end the Halloween day. Well, Lewis is always seen with Sally, Beth, Mitchell and Jacob. He now believes what he has been told about monsters.

Dracula, the Mummy and their son the Rong-a long lived together at the Count's place with Shrubs occasionally visiting them. The kids are not left out of the occasional visit to the Count's place.

THE END

www.ingramcontent.com/pod-product-compliance
Lightning Source LLC
Chambersburg PA
CBHW071251150726
48001CB00018B/1080